I read this book all by myself

....

Ahem!

To my brother, Rory

A Red Fox Book

Published by Random House Children's Books
61-63 Uxbridge Road, London W5 5SA
A division of the Random House Group Ltd

Addresses for companies within The Random House Group Limited
can be found at : www.randomhouse.co.uk/offices.htm

3 5 7 9 10 8 6 4 2

First published in Great Britain by Red Fox 2001

Published in hardback by Heinemann Library, a division of
Reed Educational and Professional Publishing Limited,
by arrangement with Random House Children's Books

Printed in Singapore by Tien Wah Press

THE RANDOM HOUSE GROUP Limited Reg. No. 954009
www.randomhouse.co.uk

ISBN 978 0 09 941726 2

All the Little Ones

and a Half

Mary Murphy

RED FOX

Here are all the little Ones.

Oh, yes. Here are all the little Ones
and a Half. I always forget the Half.

All the little Ones and a Half live in a little house. There are seven little Ones and a Half.

They are the same size as each other...

Except me— I'm only half as big.

... and they do the same work as each other.

Except me— I'm only half as strong.

They have a peaceful life.

All the little Ones love visitors.

Sorry. All the little Ones and
a Half love visitors.

Sometimes a number Two goes by, and
sometimes a number Three. The little Ones
make jugs of Oodlefizz for their visitors.

Very big numbers never pass by.
Very big numbers are scary.

One morning One looked out.

"Hey, every One!" he said. "Something funny is happening."

All the little Ones looked out.

(I haven't forgotten Half –
she just wasn't tall
enough to see out.)

Some One **could**
lift me!

11

So One lifted Half to see.

Every One saw Twos and Threes passing.

"Hey, Two! Want a drink of Oodlefizz?"
called One.

EVERY ONE
IS EQUAL

"Can't stop," said Two. "There's a big number coming this way. A big, bad number!"

"How big and bad?" asked One.

"Very big and very bad!" shouted Two.

Hurry! To the wood!

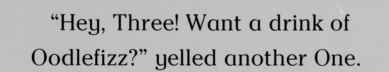

"Hey, Three! Want a drink of
Oodlefizz?" yelled another One.

"Can't stop," said Three. "There's a
big number coming this way!
A big, bad number!"

"How big and bad?" asked One.

"So big he can't walk under trees," said Three. "So bad he wants to get us! We're going to hide in the wood."

You should come too!

"I'm staying," said One. "I love our home."
Every One agreed. They locked the door
and waited.

"I can feel the house shaking," said One.
A lamp fell.

"Hey, that mountain is moving!"
said One by the window.

"That's not a mountain," said another
One. "That's the big, bad number, coming
this way!"

The big, bad number
came closer and closer.
Soon he was right at the end of
the path. His shadow was like night.

"THIS IS MY HOUSE NOW,"

roared the big, bad number.

"It belongs to every One here,"
called One out of the window.

"IT'S MINE!"

roared the big, bad
number.

Some Ones went out to talk to the big, bad number.

"You can't just take our home!" said One.

"YES, I CAN.

YOU'RE ONLY LITTLE ONES.

I'M A

HUNDRED!"

A HUNDRED!
There were seven little
Ones (and a Half). They
were not strong enough
for a Hundred.

The little Ones ran back inside.
"What will we do?" they asked.

"Ahem," said Half. "I have half an idea.
We'll go to the wood and bring back lots of
numbers. So many that all together we will
be bigger than a Hundred!"

"Yes!" cried all the little Ones. "Let's go!"

All the little Ones and a Half
sneaked out the back door. They
ran to the wood, where
the other numbers
were hiding.

Sssh!

"The Hundred has taken our house!"
they shouted.

"Oh, no!" cried all the other numbers.

"But we have an idea," said Half.

"We can count ourselves. All together
we may be as big as the Hundred."

"Good idea," said Five. "I'm the biggest
here. I'll do the counting."

27

Five set up a chart with a hundred squares. The numbers made a line.

Five filled in one square for every One.

He filled in two squares for every Two.

He filled in three squares for every Three.

He filled in four squares for every Four.

Finally, he filled in five squares for himself.

"The chart is full," said Five. "We are exactly a Hundred. We are not bigger or smaller than the Hundred. We are equal!"

"What now?" asked One.

"Now we know we're as big as the Hundred," said Five. "Let's try to get your house back."

"Wait! You forgot me again!" said Half.

"I'm only a Half, but I count too."

"You're right," said Five. "So really we all make a Hundred and a Half. We aren't equal to the Hundred . . ."

All together the numbers walked back to the little Ones' house. The big, bad Hundred was sitting on the roof.

"WHAT DO YOU WANT?"

he roared.

"WE WANT THE HOUSE BACK!" roared every One (and Two and Three and Four and Five – and a Half).

"I'M BIGGER THAN YOU,"

shouted the Hundred.

"AND I SAY IT'S MY HOUSE!"

"YOU'RE NOT BIGGER!" shouted the other
numbers. "COUNT US!"

So the Hundred did.

"One, two, three..." all the way to

"... one hundred."

"WELL," said the Hundred. "WE'RE EQUAL. YOU'LL HAVE TO FIGHT ME!"

"Ahem," said Half,
"I think you forgot me."

"YOU'RE TOO SMALL TO COUNT!" said the Hundred.

"We all count," said Half. "We all make a difference. A Hundred and a Half is bigger than a Hundred."

Ahem!

The Hundred knew that Half was right. He went away, far away.

"Hurray for Half!" shouted every One (and Two and Three and Four and Five).

And no One ever
forgot Half again.

The Numbers are having a day out. Join in the fun and help Half count.

2. Who will win the tug of war? Can you make the teams equal?

3. Numbers adding up to eight are allowed on the rafts.

Rory

Me!

Meet the author.

Mary Murphy

Where do you live? I live in Galway, Ireland.

How did you get the idea for this story? I often get ideas from my friends and family. My brother, Rory, was talking about maths and things being equal when the idea for *All the Little Ones – and a Half* started. The tricky thing was to make it work properly like maths and at the same time make it a fun story about everyone being counted.

What do you like to draw most? Animals – I have two dogs, Sally and Jem. Sometimes I put one of them into a made-up story. I loved drawing the little Ones and the other numbers. It was like drawing aliens. I don't really like drawing people. I'm not very good at it.

What did you use to make the pictures in this book? I used black Indian ink and brushes for the drawing. Then I put the colour in on the computer.

That tickles!

ink

What's your favourite place to draw?
I draw at my desk in my workroom, looking over the garden. My dogs come and sleep on blankets on the floor and listen to the radio.

What do you do if you get stuck on a drawing?
My favourite thing to do is to go for a walk with Sally and Jem, and get far away from the picture I am drawing. Or sometimes I just hide the drawing from myself, and start on a different page.

What did you like to do when you were a child? What did you hate most? I have five brothers and sisters, and all six of us loved drawing. There was lots of drawing and reading in the house. I also liked playing outdoor games like cowboys, where you were someone exciting. But I hated board games, like Monopoly, and I hated wearing dresses.

Will you try and write or draw a story?

Jem

Let your ideas take flight with
Flying Foxes

All the Little Ones – and a Half
by Mary Murphy

Sherman Swaps Shells
by Jane Clarke and Ant Parker

Digging for Dinosaurs
by Judy Waite and Garry Parsons

Shadowhog
by Sandra Ann Horn and Mary McQuillan

The Magic Backpack
by Julia Jarman and Adriano Gon

Jake and the Red Bird
by Ragnhild Scamell and Valeria Petrone